GRANDMA'S
STORIES

AWESOME

6-in-1 Series
Awesome Grandma's Stories

ISBN: 978-93-5049-408-0

Printed in 2019

© Shree Book Centre

Series editor
Sunita Pant Bansal

Published by

Shree Book Centre
8, Kakad Industrial Estate, S. Keer Marg, off L. J. Road
Matunga (west), Mumbai 400 016, India
Tel: +91-22-2437 7516 / 2437 4559 / 2438 0907
Fax: +91-22-2430 9183
Email: sales@shreebookcentre.com
Website: **www.shreebookcentre.com**

Contents

Preface

Children always long for their grandma's cheerful smiles, warm hugs and awesome stories. The joy of listening to grandma's stories is unmatched even today. These stories refresh the mind and create wonderful memories.

This book is a compilation of popular stories from around the world, often narrated by grandmothers. Written in simple language, the stories teach children important life lessons. Speech bubbles and colourful illustrations add flavour to the stories. The glossary at the end of the book will enrich the vocabulary of children.

The tales in this book will transport children to a wonderland where birds and animals talk, goodness overcomes follies, and fantasy meets reality. Let their imagination grow with these fascinating stories.

The Merchant's Secret

Once upon a time, there lived a rich merchant who travelled a lot on business. On one such trip, he helped an old woman by giving her some food and water. The old woman was actually a fairy in disguise, who wanted to test him.

The fairy was pleased with the merchant's kindness. She said, "You respect and care for old people. So, I will give you a special power that will help you understand the language of birds and animals. With this power, you will be able to help them. But, remember, you cannot tell anyone about this or else you will turn into a stone."

The merchant thanked the fairy and went home happily. With great difficulty, he managed to keep his power a secret for a long time.

One day, when the merchant and his wife were having lunch, he saw an ant picking up a few grains of rice that he had dropped around his plate. He sat there quietly, watching the little ant at work.

As the ant busily carried the rice grains, she met another ant on the way.

The other ant said, "Dear friend, give me a few rice grains and get some more for yourself. My feet are very dirty and it would be rude to walk up to the merchant's plate with such feet."

The first ant said, "If you need grains, go and get them yourself. No one will notice your dirty feet. Do you think I carry rice grains for the entire colony of ants?"

The merchant, who was listening to the conversation, could not help but laugh. His wife was offended. She said, "Why are you laughing at me? Do I look funny today?"

The merchant told her that he was not laughing at her.

His wife said, "If you did not laugh at me, then whom did you laugh at? There is no one here."

The merchant insisted, "I promise that I was not laughing at you."

But wife was not convinced and asked him to tell her why he had laughed.

She said, "You must be sick or mad to laugh without a reason."

Soon the merchant and his wife began to fight.

Their fight went on for several days, with the wife urging the merchant to tell her the truth. The merchant was fed up of this.

He thought, "I have lived my life to the fullest. My children are doing well. I have nothing to worry about. Let me tell my wife about my power. Life is hardly worth living with her annoying me day and night. But I won't tell her the truth at home. Let me take her to the river and explain everything to her. So that, when I turn into a stone, I can gently roll into the bottom of the

I will tell my wife about my powers.

river and stay there peacefully, undisturbed."

The merchant told his wife that he would take her to the river and reveal everything to her there. On their way to the river, they took a break at a well to drink some water. Here the merchant saw two goats arguing about something.

The goat's wife asked the goat to bring her a few green leaves that had grown inside the well.

The goat replied, "How can I get them for you without falling and drowning in the well? I am not as stupid as the merchant here who is about to sacrifice his life for his wife."

Saying so, the goat pushed his wife slightly. The goat's wife realized that her demand was stupid and apologized to her husband.

The goats were actually fairies who had come there to save the merchant from dying.

The merchant understood the hidden meaning of the goats' conversation and laughed. His wife looked at him suspiciously.

He said, "Did you see that? The goat got angry when his wife acted silly. I too get irritated when you keep asking me the same questions. Just believe that I have a valid reason for not answering your questions."

The merchant's wife understood what her husband meant. She went home with him quietly. The merchant and his wife never had unnecessary arguments from that day onwards. They both lived happily ever after.

Moral: Don't be foolish and give in to silly demands.

The Five Gifted Sons

Once upon a time, there lived an old man with his five sons. The boys had no mother. The old man raised them with a lot of love and care. The five sons looked alike and were gifted with strange abilities.

The eldest son could swallow the sea, the second son could not be cut by steel or iron, the third son could grow his legs and hands long, the fourth son could not be burnt by fire, and the fifth son could hold his breath indefinitely. The old man and his sons kept these strange gifts a secret from everyone.

One day, the neighbours noticed that the eldest son was going home with a lot of fish. They asked him, "How do you manage to catch so many fish? Please teach our boys to fish like you." The eldest son refused to take the neighbours' boys with him because he feared that they would find out that he swallowed the sea and took the fish from the bottom of the sea.

The neighbours were insistent and sent their boys to the sea with the eldest son. On reaching the seashore, the eldest son said, "I will suck the sea in my mouth. You boys go in and gather the fish from the bottom."

The boys went in. But they became so fascinated with the sea creatures and the corals at the bottom that they did not return for a

long time. The eldest son signalled to the boys to come back, but they did not pay heed to him. He could not hold the sea water in his mouth any longer and let it out. The boys nearly drowned.

The eldest son went back and told his neighbours what had happened. They did not believe him and accused him of trying to kill their boys.

They took him to the judge. The eldest son explained what had happened. But the judge was not satisfied with his explanation. He declared him to be guilty and passed a sentence that his head be cut off.

The eldest son pleaded with the judge, "Please let me visit my old father and my younger brothers before you punish me."

The judge granted him his last wish. The eldest son went home and told his family what had happened. The second son came up with an idea and said, "Brother, we all look alike. So, let me go in your place. Nothing can happen to me, as no steel or iron can harm me."

The brothers agreed to this and sent the second son to the judge. The executioner took out his sword and struck a mighty blow, but the sword broke. He tried again and failed again. So, the judge ordered that the second son be drowned in the sea.

The second son pleaded with the judge, "I want to take my father's blessings and let him know that I am being drowned in the sea."

The judge agreed to let him go home.

Now, the third son was sent to the judge.

He grew his legs so long that they touched the bottom of the sea and his head remained above the water.

Now, the puzzled judge ordered that he be boiled in hot oil. Once again, on the third son's plea, the judge sent him home.

Now, the fourth son was sent to the judge. He could not be burnt by fire. So, when he was put into a huge pan of boiling oil, he remained unharmed.

The judge finally decided to bury him under the ground.

With the judge's permission, the fourth son went home to meet his family. The fifth son went to the judge in his place. He was buried deep under the ground. But he could live without air. He waited till midnight and then crawled out quietly.

Thus, the five brothers helped each other and lived happily ever after.

Moral: Stay united during times of trouble.

The Crab and the Selfish Monkey

Once upon a time, there lived a crab in a hole under a plum tree, on the shady side of a mountain. The crab was hard-working and kept her hole clean. She took pride in the fact that no one in the mountain had a home like hers.

One day, the crab saw a few groundnuts on the ground, probably dropped by someone who had stopped by the tree to eat a meal. The crab became very happy and began to carry the groundnuts to her hole. A monkey who lived on the sunny side of the mountain saw the crab with the groundnuts.

His mouth watered at the sight of the groundnuts, as this was his favourite food. He thought of a plan. He said slyly to the crab, "Dear crab, will you give me half of the groundnuts in exchange for a handful of sweet plum fruits?" The crab knew that the monkey was selfish and cunning, but she agreed to his deal.

The monkey could not believe his ears and said, "Thank you so much." He quickly took the groundnuts from the crab. But he did not bother to give the crab any plum. He ran away and was not to be seen for many days.

One morning, when the crab was sitting under the plum tree, the monkey came there. This time, he wanted to eat some plums. He said to the crab, "Your tree has delicious plums. I am very hungry. Can I have some plums?"

The crab knew that the monkey had forgotten all about his deal to give her plums in exchange for groundnuts. Still she said, "Sure! You go up. Eat a few plums and throw down a few for me, as I cannot climb the tree."

The greedy monkey climbed up the tree and started eating the plums.

He kept jumping from branch to branch, plucking the ripe plums and popping them into his mouth. He did throw down a few plums for the crab, but they were either unripe or rotten. The crab was furious and called out to the monkey, "You are an ungrateful animal!"

But the monkey paid no attention to the crab.

The crab realized that there was no use scolding the selfish monkey. So, she tried to trick him. She flattered him by saying, "Oh, monkey! Now that you have eaten to your fill, I am sure you will not be able to do one of your famous somersaults."

The proud monkey wanted to prove the crab wrong and immediately went head over heels

three times. As he did so, the plums he was holding fell down to the ground. The crab quickly collected the plums and carried them home.

When the crab came back for some more plums, the angry monkey pounced on her and beat her up. When his arms started aching, he let go of the poor crab and went his way.

Luckily, the crab's friends came to her aid. The woodpecker took her home. The bee and the frog took care of her. When the crab narrated her story to her friends, they were very angry with the monkey and decided to teach him a lesson.

After a few days, the monkey returned to the plum tree.

The bee buzzed around his eyes. When the monkey was distracted, the woodpecker pecked all over his body. The monkey shouted in pain and ran away. Meanwhile, the crab had dug a deep hole in the ground. The frog sat near the opening of the hole and croaked.

Hearing the frog croak, the monkey thought that there was water nearby. But he could not see clearly, as the woodpecker had pecked him hard.

The monkey fell into the hole that the crab had dug and got hurt very badly. Thus, he was taught a good lesson for being selfish.

Moral: Do not be selfish. Learn to share.

The Mouse, the Walnut and the Mole

Long long ago, there lived a mouse with his little sister, in a small house on a tree. The mouse was very curious and adventurous. One day, he was playing in the grass when he found a walnut. He said, "Wow! What a beautiful walnut! I will take it for my little sister."

When the mouse tried to grab the walnut in his tiny paws, it slipped and fell. The walnut started rolling away from him. The mouse ran after it, saying, "Oh, my walnut! I will surely get you."

The walnut came to a big tree. It rolled under the tree's big roots and fell into a hole.

The mouse thought, "I can crawl through the hole and get back the walnut."

He peeped into the hole and saw a few small steps inside. He heard the walnut roll down the steps.

The mouse climbed down the steps and found a door at the end. He wondered who lived there.

Before the mouse could reach the walnut, the nut banged against the door. The door opened and the walnut rolled inside. The mouse quickly ran after the walnut, and the door shut after him.

The mouse was in a strange-looking room. A big mole stood in front of him. He started laughing and said, "I will keep you as my prisoner and you will work for me." The surprised mouse said, "Why would you do that? I just came looking for my walnut."

The mole said angrily, "It is my walnut now! It rolled into my house and it is mine! You will never see it again!"

The mouse was frightened and wanted to go back home. He looked all around the room, but he could not find the walnut.

He tried to run back but the door was locked.
The mole laughed and said, "There is no escape. You will live with me and work for me now. You will make my bed, sweep the floor and cook for me."

So, the poor mouse became the mole's servant.

Every day, he made the mole's bed, swept his room and cooked for him. The mouse was sad and longed to get back home. He thought of his little sister and wondered what she was doing.

The mole went away every morning and came back in the afternoon. He would lock up the mouse in his house and carry the key with him.

One day, the mole was in a hurry and forgot to lock the door. The mouse saw that the door was not locked. This was the perfect chance to escape. But he wanted to take the walnut with him.

The mouse did not know where the mole had kept the walnut. He looked for it everywhere—in the cupboard, on every shelf and in the drawers.

But he did not find the walnut anywhere. Finally, he looked in the tiny chimney. He exclaimed, "There you are, my precious walnut!"

The mouse took the walnut and ran as fast as he could, past the door, up the steps and through the hole in the tree, till he reached his house.

"Brother!" his sister cried joyfully, throwing her arms around his neck. She said, "I'm so glad to see you, my sweet brother. Where did you go? You have no idea know how much I missed you!"

The mouse calmed her down and narrated all that had happened to him.

Then he placed the walnut on a table and opened it. Lo and behold! There was a tiny ring inside! The mouse gave the ring to his sister. She loved it.

The mole could never find the mouse or the walnut ever again.

Moral: Be patient and think with a calm and clear mind.

The Kind Dwarf and the Enchanted Castle

Once upon a time, there lived a peasant with his three sons. The youngest son was a dwarf.

One day, the three brothers left home to find their fortune. After a while, they came across an anthill. The eldest brother said, "Let's destroy the anthill and watch the ants run."

The dwarf said, "No, brothers! Please let the poor things enjoy themselves. I will not let you trouble them."

His two brothers laughed at this. But they did not harm the ants. Then they left the place.

After some time, they came to a lake with many ducks.

The second brother said, "Let us roast two ducks and eat them for dinner."

But the dwarf stopped him and said, "No! We have enough food. Let the ducks enjoy themselves. Do not kill them."

The brothers moved on from there.

Next, they came to a beehive inside a tree.

There was a lot of honey in the tree. The two elder brothers said, "Let us light a fire and kill the bees. And then we can take the honey." But the dwarf held them back and said, "No! Please let the pretty bees enjoy themselves. I won't let you burn them."

After a long time, the three brothers reached
an enchanted castle. There seemed to be no one
there. The brothers saw many marble statues in
the castle grounds. They explored all the rooms
in the castle. Finally, they came to a room where
an old man was sitting at a table.

"Excuse us, kind man," said the eldest brother.
The old man did not hear him.

The eldest brother called him a couple of times more, but the old man still did not hear him. Then the three brothers called out together. The old man heard them and walked towards them. Without saying a word, he led them to a beautiful table laid with various foods and drinks. After they had eaten, he showed them to the bedrooms.

The next morning, the old man took the eldest brother to a marble table. There were three tablets on it. The tablets bore the instructions to break the spell surrounding the castle. The first tablet said, "In the forest, under the moss, lie a thousand pearls belonging to the king's daughter. They must all be found before sunset, or else he who seeks them will be turned into marble."

The eldest brother set out. By evening, he had found fewer than a hundred pearls. So, he was turned into a marble statue. The next day, the second brother undertook the task. He too could not collect all the pearls. So, he was also turned into a marble statue.

Now it was the dwarf's turn. He searched in the moss. But it was so hard to find the pearls that he sat down on a stone and cried.

But soon help arrived. The ants, whose life he had saved, helped him. They quickly found all the pearls. The dwarf took the pearls to the castle.

The next morning, the quiet old man pointed to the second tablet.

The tablet said, "The key to the princess's bedroom must be fished out of the lake."

As the dwarf stood at the edge of the lake, the two ducks whose lives he had saved dived into the water, fetched the key and gave it to him.

The third task was the hardest. The young man had to choose the youngest of the king's three daughters.

Now, they were all beautiful and looked alike. He was told that the eldest girl had eaten some sugar, the second daughter had had sweet syrup and the youngest girl a spoonful of honey. He had to guess who had eaten honey.

Just then, one of the bees whose life the dwarf had saved sat upon the lips of the princess who had eaten the honey.

The dwarf pointed out that she was the youngest daughter who had had the honey. Thus, the spell was broken and his brothers became normal.

The dwarf married the youngest princess and his brothers married the other princesses.

Moral: **Be kind to others and they will help you when in need.**

The Wise Young Man

Once there lived a wise and rich king. He had a beautiful daughter. He knew that many people would want to marry her, when she grew up, to get her wealth. So, he thought of a plan. When the princess grew up, the king built a palace under the ground and hid her inside it.

Then he sent his men all around the kingdom with this message: *Whoever finds the king's daughter shall marry her. But if someone tries and fails, then he must die.*

Many young men wanted to marry the princess. But no one had the courage to risk their lives.

Now, there was a handsome and clever young man. He had a great desire to take up this challenge.

The young man went to a shepherd. With the shepherd's help, he disguised himself in a sheepskin with golden fleece, so that he looked like a golden lamb. Then he persuaded the shepherd to take him to the king.

When the king saw the golden lamb, he asked the shepherd, "Will you sell this lamb to me?"

The shepherd said, "No, sir! I will not sell him, but I will lend him to you for three days. After that, you must return him to me."

The king agreed and took the lamb to his daughter. He led him to the underground palace, through many rooms. Then they came to a big

I want to buy this lamb.

door. The king said, "Open, Sartara Martara of Earth."

The door opened and they reached the princess's chamber, which had exquisite walls, floor and roof. The king embraced the princess and gave her the lamb. The princess was overjoyed. Then the king went away.

The princess stroked the lamb and played with him. Slowly, night fell. The young man threw away the skin. The princess was amazed to see him and fell in love with him in an instant. She then asked him, "Why did you come here disguised as a lamb?"

The man answered, "Your father has said that anyone who tries to find you but fails to do so will be killed. So, I invented this trick to come to you safely."

The princess exclaimed, "That is well done indeed! But your test is not over yet. When you tell him that you have found me, my father will turn me and my aides into ducks. And, then, he will ask you, 'Which of these ducks is the princess?' So, at that time, I will turn my head back and clean my wings with my bill, so that you know it is me."

Three days later, the shepherd came back to the king and said, "O King! I have come for my lamb."

Please give me back my lamb.

The king returned the golden lamb to the shepherd, along with a big reward.

After some time, the young man went to the king and said, "Sir, I am confident that I can find your daughter."

When the king saw how handsome he was, he said, "My lad, you seem so young. I pity you, for you will surely die trying to find my daughter."

But the young man answered, "O King, I will either find her or lose my head."

Then the young man led the king to the underground palace. Finally, they came to the princess's chamber. The young man said to the king, "Say the words that will open the door."

The king asked, "What are the words? Should I say 'open, open, open'?"

"No! Say 'open Sartara Martara of Earth'," said the young man.

The king was stunned. He said the words and the door opened. They went in and found the princess. Then the king immediately turned the princess and her aides into ducks. He pointed to the ducks and said to the young man, "Now tell me who my daughter is."

Just then, the princess began to clean her wings with her bill. The young man immediately said, "She who's cleaning her wings is the princess."

The king was happy and he married his daughter to the young man. The young man and the princess lived happily together.

Moral: Use your intelligence to overcome challenges.